A Room Full of Strangers

A Room Full of Strangers

Francis John Balducci

The Library of Congress
Control Number 1-6383473711

Balducci, Francis John, 1964–
a room full of strangers / Francis John Balducci

ISBN-13 978-0-692-09132-6
ISBN 06209132-7

Front and rear cover designs, images and elements by the author.

Printed in the United States of America.

DEDICATION

To my friend Steven "Vinyl Fatigue" Levy
of Long Beach, New York.

An idea, like a ghost, must be spoken with a little before it will explain itself.

Charles Dickens

PROLOGUE

Laura Bennings is a careful driver.

The white lines of the open New England highway move steadily beneath her wheels. The young woman changes lanes only when necessary, and she never exceeds the speed limit.

Her small New Hampshire-bound sedan is packed to its ceiling with her belongings. Clothing, papers, and other items are tightly jammed in cardboard boxes and milk crates. Some soil has spilled on the front-passenger seat from a tilted planter that holds a small, wilting philodendron. But, she has no worries. A song from The Guess Who blares from the dashboard speakers. She holds the steering wheel firmly with the exception of an index finger that taps to the rhythm of the song.

"No time left for you..." she sings.

Tall greenery lines the highway on both sides. Over the distant horizon, rain clouds loom low in the springtime sky and threaten to release a deluge upon the dry asphalt.

With every passing mile, Philadelphia is becoming more of a distant memory to Laura. She is breaking free—stepping out of the shadows of the legacy of her affluent family, and her timing could not be any better: A prestigious career with Westry Technologies in Concord awaits her—a profession that will put her extensive marketing education and work experience to good use. It is her intense yearning to be independently successful, and to perhaps meet the right man, settle down and start a family of her own.

For years she half-jokingly referred to her step-father's wealth as "*his* money." She continues to feel this way two years after his death. Although it is tempting to use some of that money to immediately pay off the remainder of her college debt—even at the insisting of her loving, overly-protective mother—she stubbornly will not take a cent. She has some savings—tens of thousands in the bank; some of it is a pay advance from her new employer.

Laura deeply loves her mother. But, she had no hesitation to leave her after being thoroughly convinced that the woman will be fine without her. More importantly, she needed to free herself from a huge mansion of empty rooms where she sees herself wasting away to nothing. Laura's move is her call to adventure, and she has never been more excited.

She looks at the dashboard digital clock. She then looks up at the storm in the far-off distance.

Realizing that she is making good time, she exits the highway to call her mother.

* * *

"Yes, mom, I'm almost there.... I'll call you tonight from the hotel.... I love you, too. Bye, mom."

As Laura closes her cell phone, she decides to find a place to eat. She continues driving down a narrowing road for a half mile. She notices a change in the environment go from an open landscape to a quaint, cozy town.

A lone restaurant appears in the distance. A bulky, wooden sign hangs over the front doorway bearing the name, "Waterside Pub." She parks and goes inside.

"Sit anywhere!" an unseen woman bellowed from deep inside the place. Laura takes a menu and sits at a booth. Surrounding her is the strong smell of sour beer. In the distance, she hears a progressive British-rock song over a low-volume jukebox. Looking up, she is reminded of her high school history class when she sees a framed black-and-white print of Franklin Pierce. The president's image is squarely hung over a stone fireplace. She also notices a bar in the distance. The waitress appears.

"Specials today are roast turkey or meatloaf, and today's soup is Yankee bean," the waitress said while staring the entire time at her check pad. Laura notices the wrinkles and age spots on the woman's hands.

"*Yankee bean*—really? Of course Yankee bean." Laura said jokingly and innocently.

The waitress just looks at her while Laura's smile slowly disappears.

"Ah, turkey, but no soup." Laura said as she straightens up in her seat and returns the menu.

Just then, a commotion breaks out at the bar. She hears a few men talking rather irately. An older man, frustrated and forgetful that he is in a public place, shouts at another man.

"The house at Seven Oaks is a *murder* house—I'm telling you! The place is *damned!*"

Upon hearing this, the other man quickly storms out. The older man turns back to the bar.

"That man is doomed," he said while picking up his beer. He takes a sip and gulps. "He's *doomed.*"

* * *

Later that night, Laura nestles into her hotel room. She is somewhere in a suburb of Concord, about ten miles from the city. She plans on staying in this room for a few weeks until she settles into her new career and purchases a home.

As she readies for bed, she intently watches the news to learn more about her fresh surroundings. There's low crime, cold weather, and a new cookie shop that opened on the eastside of town.

Within an hour, Laura is asleep. The television continues to display imagines—this time, the screen shows two ladybugs in courtship.

ONE

The seven-spotted ladybug has a lifespan of approximately one month. In a suburban environment, it will live out its entire life within an area no larger than a square mile.

There are those who believe that the tiny existence of the seven-spotted ladybug is highly inconsequential to the entire planet. Notwithstanding, the collective species—with over millions of years of evolution and after undergoing very few physiological changes—has in fact managed to make a significant impact on global ecological systems.

* * *

Laura adequately contains her enthusiasm during her morning routine. Skincare, makeup, and hair, all done while she ponders on how to make a favorable first impression. She rehearses in the mirror. In the next room, a tailor-made executive business suit is carefully laid out on the bed next to a half-eaten bagel and a small orange. The clock radio blaringly offers the local traffic report.

She emerges from the bathroom, partially nude and looking well made up. She finishes her tea at the nightstand. She dresses in the suit, which fits her perfectly. She carefully slips on a pair of Christian Louboutin pumps. She then stuffs work papers into a large leather bag. When she leaves, she purposely keeps the clock radio on. After a quick stop at the concierge, she decides to leave her car and take the bus.

Even though it is early May, Laura feels a winter chill on her nose and lips. Yet, she does not mind. She walks to the main street and pans around until she sees the eastbound bus stop. The bus quickly arrives before she can cross. She hurries while it waits for her.

While inside, she smiles at the driver. He smiles back with a broad grin. She scans the other passengers while keeping her smile, and then she takes a seat.

For a few minutes, she gazes at the life around her though the huge window. She notices all the people moving about at a steady pace, and no one appears to be rushing in any way. She then opens her bag and starts reading from some of the papers. It is not long before she hears the driver call out.

"Whittendam Street, Westry Building!"

Laura jumps to her feet so quickly that she accidentally drops the papers that she was holding.

She hurries to pick them up while the driver speaks to her in a gentle voice.

"You take your time, miss. I'll keep the door open for you."

She ably collects her things and springs out of the bus. She turns to wave at the driver to gesture her thanks, but the man already pulled away.

* * *

A ladybug slowly crawls across a slate sidewalk. Before it can reach the safety of a small crack, it is unintentionally crushed by the pump that Laura is wearing. The poor creature's yellowed entrails exhibit a gooey glisten on the stone surface.

Laura quickly crosses a wide street and steps onto a bright sidewalk. She detects the smells of coffee and baked goods. Beyond some fellow commuters, she encounters some food venders and a newspaper stand. She also notices something that seems rather out of place: It is a white-faced mime artist performing his act. He stops, looks at her, smiles, and then pantomimes the tipping of a hat. Laura smiles back and then gazes around the grand entrance to Westry Plaza. She enters the grounds.

In the plaza, she looks up at a sculpture of a large "W" that sits atop of a massive iron globe. A biomechanical-inspired design representing all of the continents was skillfully etched onto its surface.

Beyond the plaza, Laura sees the Westry Building. It reaches so high that it nearly disappears into a hovering cloud. Its structure is narrow, with clean lines, black windows, and blueish steel trusses that rise and crisscross every seven floors. As the clouds move off, a golden spire of glass proudly appears, which the building wears like a royal crown. She hurries to the main entrance.

While inside the lobby, Laura sees retail stores, a florist, and a barbershop. Beyond a threshold, she sees a wide atrium boasting multi-colored marble floors, gray marble walls, lighting that runs up the walls and across the ceilings, and a massive waterfall sculpture framed with tall greenery on both sides. Grand escalators on either side support the architectural symmetry. Emerald green elevator doors are situated ahead. The sign that reads, "Floors 37–ES" illuminates, and the well-detailed doors open for Laura.

"Floor, ma'am?" asked the elevator operator.

"Executive suite, please."

The doors close.

* * *

Nathaniel Westry's secretary sits smartly at her desk. Laura approaches her while wearing a nervous smile.

"May I help you?" the secretary asked.

"My name is Laura Bennings, and I'm here to see Mr. Westry."

"Yes, Miss Bennings, Mr. Westry is expecting you. You are right on time. Please follow me." She stands revealing her tall, sleek physique, and walks behind a tall yucca plant in the corner of the room.

"Come right this way," she said.

Laura looks slightly confused at the woman. The secretary pushes on the wall to open a panel revealing a hidden staircase. Laura carefully follows her up the steps. The solid door at the top is opened wide to reveal an impressive room. Black and gold checker floors glisten below her while black marble walls rise up supporting a golden, glass spire above them. An old, well-dressed gentleman slowly rises from a majestic desk.

"Laura Bennings!" he said cheerfully.

The secretary quickly turns and leaves.

"Good morning, Mr. Westry," Laura said with a trembling voice.

"Please, call me Nate." He walks to her. "It's great to see Gerald's daughter all grown up."

"You knew my step-father?"

"*Everyone* in the business world knew your father. Here..." He walks over to the wall of framed photographs. "That's a much-younger me standing with him." He sighs. "He was a powerful titan, and a personal mentor."

Laura notices on another wall several framed photographs of Westry standing with politicians and other business people. The photos include one with casino mogul Ronald Drake.

"I didn't know that you knew Gerald," she said with a hint of disappointment.

"Now, let me assure you of something: You were hired because of your very impressive credentials. You come highly recommended by Global Dynamics, and I've known Jeremy Tyler there for decades. So, you have a lot to offer this company, and that's the only reason why you're here. Okay? Say, why don't you see your new office and get settled. My secretary, Carol, will show you around."

* * *

The offices of Westry Technologies have glass walls everywhere. The atmosphere seems slightly unsettling with mirror effects and eyes watching your every move. The smells of carpeting and brewing coffee pervade the halls and office areas, and they unleash an assault on Laura's senses. Still, her enthusiasm and excitement allow her to ignore this distraction.

People smile at Laura as she is introduced to them. A smile never leaves her face as she glides along from person to person, from smiling face to smiling face.

While at her office, she looks over a rough schedule and some assignments. Later in the day, she attends an executive meeting. After lunch, she attends another meeting, and then she conducts an interview for the graphic arts division. All went smoothly, with the exception of a technological glitch that she has been experiencing with her office e-mail account.

A mid-level information-technology technician reports to Laura's office. He peers through the doorway and speaks to her with a soft voice.

"Miss Bennings? You requested IT?"

"Yes, c'mon in. I can't gain access to my e-mail and, when I do, it logs me out."

"I see. That's a simple fix. I just need to sit at your work station," he said without making eye contact with her.

"Well, it's all yours." Laura looks at him, smiles, and gestures to the computer.

Without hesitation, Evan takes out a small bottle of hand sanitizer and rigorously rubs the liquid on his hands until it thoroughly evaporates. He then tucks in his periwinkle shirt and adjusts his collar before he sits. On the monitor, he opens a black screen with green letters, he types a line of letters and numbers, and then he presses "enter."

"All done."

"All done?" she asked almost cheerfully. "That's it?"

"That's it. Your computer is new and I needed to synchronize it with our e-mail system," he said while still not making eye contact with her.

"It sounds very complicated," she said playfully.

"Oh, not really. It's rather simple."

"What is your name?"

"Evan."

"Evan?"

"Evan Platt." He looks into her eyes briefly and offers her a tiny smile.

"Well, Evan Platt, it's nice to meet you. Please call me Laura."

"All right, Laura." Evan's smile broadens. "Well, I must be off. I never know when they'll need me, you know," he said somewhat awkwardly. His quick exit abruptly ends the conversation.

Laura wonders about Evan's shyness and whether he struggles for acceptance. Some may find his actions rude, but she understands him. She considers her own awkwardness around people. She perhaps sees in him the same vulnerabilities that she sees within herself. More importantly, she regards his smile to be the most genuine one that she has received all day.

* * *

After a few weeks of tireless searching, Laura finds her perfect house in the small, suburban town of Harrogate. It is a quaint yet sturdy wood-framed structure not far from the main road.

Some may regard the place as inauspicious. But, Laura sees great potential; she enters each room imagining the right furnishings and decorations. She opens a closet, and she is instantly spooked when a cicada flies out. After she quickly regains her composure, she continues brainstorming for some ideas.

Not long after her home receives a bed, drapes, and some furniture, Laura receives a visit from her mother, Julia.

"Darling, you're losing too much weight." She enters while carrying a few wrapped bundles.

"Mom, I'm fine. And, what's with the truck and the moving men?"

"I thought I'd bring some things from home—some things I think you need."

The men carefully haul a bulky, wooden mass from a truck.

"What? You brought me the piano?"

"It's *your* piano—you're the only one who plays it." She reacts to Laura's disapproval. "Well, you can *try* to thank me."

"Okay, thank you."

Julia looks around the house. "Are you happy here?"

"I'm happy. I'm making friends at work. The community is rather quiet and to itself, but I'm happy here."

"You can always stop this experiment and come home."

"Mother, this is not an experiment, and this *is* my home."

"And must you drive that car? Let me buy you a new one, something safer. BMWs are nice. A Cadillac?"

"I'm fine with my car. No."

Julia draws in a breath. "You know, the boy you used to like is back from college. He graduated and he's home for good."

"That was years ago. I moved on. I'm sure he moved on, too."

"He's not seeing anyone."

"Trust me, we both moved on." Laura takes a deep breath. "This is my home now, mother. I want to make this work. I'm going to make this work."

"Well, okay.   Anyway, I brought you some housewarming gifts. Here..."

Julia hands Laura one wrapped package. Laura tears away the paper to reveal a silver serving tray.

"And here are some frankincense candles for the house." She then takes out a flat object loosely wrapped in newspaper and hands it to Laura. Laura unwraps it.

"A plaque, mother? Really?" Laura holds it up.

"Yes, and I want you to hang it above the main entrance. See? It reads,

'Home is the best place to be

No matter where it happens to be.' "

Two

The fresh coat of exterior house paint glistens and reflects the July sunset.

"The place is coming together," Laura thinks as she glares at the happy façade. The old house has a breath of new life and, with paint smudges on her face, she holds no shame for admiring her handiwork and color choices.

Overall, the house undergoes a few renovations especially in the major rooms of the house, such as the kitchen. New appliances catapult Laura into the twenty-first century. She considers entertaining guests with the addition of new furniture in the parlor.

The landscaping work included the removal of dead scrubs and the planting of several flowering bushes. Laura's new car is perched in the freshly-graveled driveway. Next to the car sits a stout, wooden post. A birdhouse that Laura ably constructed from leftover materials is sturdily fixed to it. The colors of the birdhouse match those of the master house thus rendering it as a near-perfect miniaturized copy. Laura intended this. She watches the tiny home and wonders how long it will remain vacant.

* * *

Laura quickly adapts to her new work environment. She has made many favorable impressions. Also, her office is physically taking shape. Degrees and awards from Temple University prominently hang above a table with track-and-field trophies neatly arranged on it. Inhabiting her desktop include a few other awards, a small globe, and a half-eaten Chinese lunch. In the center of these items is a small, carefully giftwrapped box.

The IT department is the only major office of Westry Technologies that is located in the basement. It is well isolated from the rest of the building for reasons that leave some to humorously speculate. Down a long labyrinth of cables and colored wires, beyond a vast computer system and a door that bears his name, Evan Platt quietly sits inside. His desk is well cluttered. His eyes dart across large monitors perched side by side that display various images and characters. Covering much of the gray walls hang several horror and science-fiction movie posters and other memorabilia from those genres.

After Laura enters the basement, she passes by a large, chrome machine adorned with screens and colored lights. She approaches Evan's door and knocks on it. It slowly opens. Evan offers her a somewhat surprised look.

"Hi, Evan."

"Hi."

"I just wanted to stop by and give you a little something." She hands him the small box.

"Um, why?"

"Because I thought you were very helpful and I want to show you my appreciation."

Evan opens the box and takes out a small figurine of a smiling man leaning against an oversized computer. "Oh, thanks."

As he tries to find a place to put it, Laura looks around his office.

"So, Evan, what do you do exactly?"

"I do several things like help good people like you."

Laura smiles at him.

"But, specifically, I work on gaming products in the virtual reality entertainment line, or VRE. That's what I specialize in."

"Games? That's so interesting."

"We are rapidly expanding on new gaming ideas and virtual reality technology. The work is never-ending."

"And, I see that you like horror and science fiction."

"Yeah, I'm somewhat of a fan," he said with a smile.

"Me, too. I love being creeped out."

Evan keeps his smile and looks at her. "You want to be creeped out?"

Laura laughs. "Sure. Who doesn't?"

Evan thinks for a moment. "I have something for you." He picks up a confidential report from a pile of other items and hands it to her.

"What's this?" she asked as she opens it.

"That's the newest virtual reality game created by Westry himself. It will be embedded into the dark web."

"The dark web?"

"Yes, it's a boundless area of the non-indexed web that requires special software. Here..." Evan moves some papers and finds a white disc with some writing on it. He gives it to her. "This will allow you access. Just follow the instructions."

"Tell me more about the game."

"Well, the object is for the players to fight a race of evil creatures and ultimately save the universe."

Laura takes the disc. "When will the game be available?"

"We launch it tonight to a very limited audience to test it out. It will be released to the general public in about three weeks, but you can check it out tonight before it gets crowded. It will be regarded as the most complex, most integrated, and most realistic product that Westry has ever created."

"So exciting. What is the game called?"

He pauses and looks directly into her eyes. "A Room Full of Strangers."

"Wow! Scary name."

"I know, right?" Evan gestures outside his office. "Did you see the huge computer that you passed?"

"Oh, that's a computer?" She smiles. "How could I miss it?"

"Well, she's so much more than just a computer. She manages all of our online virtual reality entertainment platforms, including this game."

"She?"

"Well, her name is Valerie."

* * *

At home, after Laura parked her car in the driveway, she notices that a chickadee had moved into her birdhouse. She smiles with excitement.

She steps inside and throws an attaché case on the couch while on her way to the kitchen to make coffee.

Upstairs, she disrobes, and playfully struts into her closet while carrying a coffee mug. She then sits at her computer to review the dating profile of a man that she will be seeing on this night. It is the first date of her new life, and she is nervous and hopeful.

* * *

The man shows up at her door. He is tall, handsome, and even better looking than his appearance in the dating profile photograph. She leaves with him without allowing him entry into her home—something that her mother taught her to always do.

After dinner and an evening of conversation, the man drives her home. At her front door, they talk a little more. When he considers the time to be right, he leans in to kiss her on her lips. She smiles and then turns her head to present her cheek to him. He disappointedly kisses her there. They both then nervously laugh at this. He tries again to kiss her on the lips. She moves her head back.

"Well," she said, "I had a great time."

"Me, too." He tries to embrace her.

"I want to take things slowly, okay?" she said as she moves back.

"C'mon, just one kiss," he softly insists as she takes out her keys.

"Please, you're a nice guy, but I'm tired and I need to go inside now."

He embraces her slightly and attempts another kiss. He moves his hands down her back and pulls her hip into his groin. She readies her handful of keys by steadily drawing them back. With one move, she strikes the man hard embedding the keys in his cheek. She withdraws them. The blood immediately flows from the deep wound as he steps back giving Laura an opportunity to escape his grip. She quickly inserts a dripping key into the lock, opens the door, and then slams the door behind her.

"Why did you do that, you fucking bitch!" he screamed.

"If you don't leave, I'll call the police. Then, you will be fucked!"

She looks outside a window to see him stumbling to his car. He quickly drives off. She sits and breaks down crying.

* * *

Later that night, after a relaxing bath, and with a hot beverage in hand, Laura attempts to enter the game that Evan talked about. Her curiosity dominates her mind. She sits at her computer and inserts the disc that he gave her. After the download, she opens the file and then runs it. She gains passage to the dark web. Admittance was easier than she anticipated as she navigates passed websites that Evan told her to avoid. She finds a special message posted with the Westry logo. There, she finds a link to the game. She sees the name, "A Room Full of Strangers," and clicks on it. She is prompted to enter an access code. She enters the one that Evan e-mailed her.

Her screen immediately goes black. Then, a pinhole of white appears in the center. It steadily morphs and swirls around getting larger and larger. Laura becomes transfixed over the anomaly. She presses the escape key. Upon doing so, she sees a large flash on the screen. It goes blank, and the computer turns off.

Laura finishes her beverage, turns the lights out, and goes to bed.

* * *

At her office, Laura feels a bit uneasy. Naturally, she is upset about the terrible ending to her date, but she is confused and uncertain about the game. She hears a knock at the open doorway.

"What did you think?"

"Evan, I couldn't get in. Did I get the correct access code?"

"Yes, I'm certain of it. What happened?"

"I'm not sure, but I saw a light getting larger and larger. I thought there was a problem, so I tried to escape it. That's when my computer turned off."

"No, let your computer run. It takes a few minutes for the game to open."

"I guess I'm impatient."

"You said you saw a light getting larger?"

She nods.

"And your computer shut down on its own?"

"Yes."

"That's odd." He thinks. "But, try again."

Before she has a chance to thank him, he is quickly on his way without speaking another word.

* * *

In the evening, Laura walks up to the birdhouse and quietly and carefully peers in. She notices that the chickadee has laid a tiny egg. This discovery fills Laura with wonderment and satisfaction. This also gives her some optimism of her own domestic prospects.

THREE

While Laura sits at her piano, she reflects on her childhood in Philadelphia. She remembers back when she was as young as four years old. She remembers summer walks with her mother. They talked about the prospect of her mother marrying Gerald Bennings. Laura then begins to play the instrument. Her hands skillfully move across the keys. She plays September Song—her step-father's favorite. He found supreme joy when she played it.

She recalls the first day her mother met this business giant, and how smitten she was with the way he walked, and spoke, and with the sort of tea that he drank. It was total. Laura remembers the first time she called him "dad." She continues to play until the doorbell rings.

Laura sees a couple and a small boy at her doorstep. The woman is carrying something wrapped in foil.

"Hi! We're the Parks family, your neighbors,"

the woman said.

"Oh, hello. My name is Laura, Laura Bennings."

"Oh, yes. We read about you in the *Harrogate News*," the man said.

"You work at Westry Technologies," the boy said.

"Yes, I do."

"Our son is only nine and already loves anything that involves computers and technology," the woman proudly said as she strokes the boy's hair. "We call him our little hacker."

"Really?" Laura smiles.

"My name is Lilian, and this is my husband, Bill, and our son, Aaron.

"Mom, the pie."

"Oh, and we baked you a pie. It's from the apples on our property, and it's sweetened with the honey from our own hives."

"That's so nice of you," Laura said while taking the pie. "I'll make coffee."

"No, thank you. We're off to church and then dinner with the in-laws. You're welcome to join us."

"Oh, no I can't. Thank you. I have to get a jump on the week," she said while gesturing to a tall stack of papers on the dining room table.

"All right, we'll see you around," Lilian said.

"Absolutely."

Bill waves and never loses his smile.

As the Parks turn to leave, Aaron hesitates. He offers Laura a soft, innocent smile. Laura smiles back. He then hurries off.

"Aaron," she thinks. "Nice kid."

* * *

The days have become shorter. Laura stands half dressed in the kitchen at the cutting board. Outside, the rain quickly helps to fill the driveway with water and mud.

She stares down at a ripened tomato. "It's perfect," she thinks as she is about to cut into it. She carefully grips the handle of the well-sharpened knife and steadily holds it. A tiny droplet of water slowly runs down to the blade's tip. She cuts downward with precision.

An image of her step-father unexpectedly flashes in her mind. He is smiling at her, waving. She sees him in the corner of her eye, in the doorway. She turns away from the cutting board. Yet, she continues to cut down, slicing. No one is there. She turns her head in the other direction to scan the room. She cuts down again while refocusing her eyes. When she returns to the cutting board, the fleshy produce appears to be bleeding out. Then, while noticing her open finger, the pain from her mishap reaches her brain.

She tightly clutches onto the wounded digit and hastens to the bathroom. She swiftly bandages the cut and then returns to the kitchen. On the cutting board, she finds the tomato sliced and neatly stacked. The knife sits without a trace of blood on its blade. In order to prevent a panic attack, Laura immediately decides to accept what she sees. With her appetite lost, she proceeds elsewhere in the house.

The floral smell of fabric softener hangs in the air of the laundry room. Laura notices that a load of clothes awaits her in the washing machine. She puts a large basket in place and carefully retrieves her laundry, one item at a time. With her task complete, she looks down with shock at her blood-stained clothes. She quickly realizes that her finger bled through the bandage. Without saying a word, Laura dumped the laundry back into the washing machine. As the machine commences with its gyrations, she commands herself to go somewhere and unwind.

She pours a glass of wine and stares at her computer from across her bedroom. As she leans forward, she misjudges the flow in her glass. The red beverage spills on the last remaining clean shirt that she is wearing.

As she rigorously wipes her shirt with a towelette, she again looks at her computer. She tosses the wipe in the wastebasket, walks over, and sits down at the keypad. She turns on the computer, and again she inserts Evan's disc. After the download, she opens the file and then runs it. She stares into the dark web and again finds the Westry logo. She clicks on the link and carefully enters the access code.

As soon as the code is entered, Laura experiences a flash of light so powerful that she is shocked and knocked to the floor unconscious.

After some time, Laura awakes. As she struggles to her feet, she realizes that blood is dripping from her nose. She quickly applies tissue to the nostrils as she attempts to compose herself. She sits back in her chair, takes a deep breath, and stares puzzled at a dead screen. While she picks up her glass to drink, she considers the possibility that perhaps the computer experienced a short circuit. She gulps the wine while nearly spilling it again.

* * *

A few hours later, before going to bed, Laura sits at the piano and plays September Song again. She thinks she is performing it correctly, but it does not sound right. She quickly discovers that some of keys may be out of tune. So, she decides to sit by the fireplace and read a book that she recently purchased from a local drug store. The story in the book interests here because it involves horrific moon creatures that invade Earth.

The candles that her mother gave her are brightly lit and perched on the mantle. Their flames flicker a few times and catch Laura's attention. She tries to detect if there is a breeze entering the room, but she determines that the air feels quite still. As she returns to her reading, the flames unexpectedly go out. She rises out of her chair and relights them. She turns back to the chair to notice that the book that she was reading has slightly moved from where she thought she placed it. She dismisses any notion that it moved on its own and regards herself as being absent-minded.

As Laura continues to read her book, she thinks

she sees shadows from the corners of her eyes. After she rubs her eyes, she decides that she is more tired than she wants to admit to herself. She then blows out the candles and heads for her bedroom.

In the bathroom, now Laura thinks she sees images in the wall mirror. She moves her head and squints and quickly sees the face of a stranger. After she blinks a few times, the face is gone. All she is left with is the disturbed look on her face staring back at her in the reflection.

* * *

Laura experiences some bizarre encounters while food shopping. As she walks down the aisles, several of her fellow shoppers blankly stare at her. On one occasion, she speaks to one shopper—an old woman—to break the woman's gaze. But, she does not answer. Instead, she turns away and swiftly walks off. While paying for her groceries, the cashier is quiet and seems emotionally removed. Laura leaves the market and quickly pushes the cart to her car in the parking lot. She hopelessly dodges the rain drops falling around her.

While driving home, the rain beats down hard on the windshield. On the side of the road, Laura sees something. It is a dog. It is thoroughly muddied and looks abandoned and alone. It is not wearing a collar. She quickly pulls over. The dog approaches Laura without any apprehension. The animal shivers as Laura takes him into her car. As it sits, it looks up at Laura and wags its tail. She covers the poor creature with a blanket.

At home, the dog curls up by the fireplace after having some of Laura's dinner. It is a rather sizable male, and he appears to be in good health. While she looks at him, she takes a shot of tequila. She looks at the label on the bottle and decides to name him Cabo. She calls to him by his new name. He lifts his head in response and he appears to smile at her.

Laura notices that she needs more firewood. She grabs a coat and goes outside to the wood shack. While there, she overhears some whispers around her. When she stops to listen, the voices stop. As she gathers up some logs in her arms, she hears more whispers. The sounds stop again when she stops moving. She then goes inside with the wood.

After Laura lit a raging fire, she tries calling her mother. However, the phone is dead. She has another shot of tequila as she watches Cabo fall asleep.

* * *

Early in the morning, Laura heads out of the house to go jogging. She brings Cabo with her with hopes that the owner may see him and reclaim him. As she runs, the dog keeps pace well and even appears to smile at her. She immediately realizes that she may be his new owner, and she welcomes that idea.

While at work, she attempts to visit with Evan. When she arrives at his office, she learns that he is home sick. Also, Valerie does not appear to be operating. She then visits the human resources office and learns Evan's home address.

After work, she goes to Evan's house for a surprise visit. While carrying a paper bag that holds a container of soup, she rings his doorbell. She labors to look through a tiny window in the door. He does not appear to be home.

* * *

While Laura enters her driveway, she notices that a sparrow now occupies the birdhouse. The creature laid eggs of her own. The chickadee, however, is gone and is nowhere to be seen.

FOUR

Halloween has arrived, and it is Laura's favorite holiday.

Scary decorations of witches and scarecrows hang in practically every window of her house. A grinning skull is affixed by a nail to the front door. At our feet, an illuminated Jack-o'-lantern offers visitors a toothy facial expression.

Inside, a sizable basket filled passed the brim with various candies sits ready by the door. Laura is prepared for anticipated trick-or-treaters.

Although she is not in costume, she reflects on her younger years when she dressed up. She was always a princess, every year, and the clothes and accessories were quite authentic and the best that money can buy.

Hours tick by, and Laura sits next to the heaping bowl of candy as it inhabits a small table. She looks at the bowl with disgust. After well into the evening, by nine o'clock, no one has rung her doorbell. She does not recall if any children had even passed in front of her house.

In the kitchen, Laura makes a cup of tea. As she takes her first sip, Cabo reacts to something at the front door. The dog cowers when someone abruptly and loudly knocks.

"Yes?"

"*Trick or treat!*" said a few muffled voices in unison.

"Oh, one moment."

Laura picks up the bowl and swings the door open. She finds herself confronted by three teenagers in masks. One of them is cradling her Jack-o'-lantern.

"Aren't you boys a little old for trick-or-treating?" she asked.

They giggle at her question and look at each other.

"What do you boys want?

After another giggle, one of them answers.

"Can-dy."

The boys laugh. One jams his door in the doorway to prevent it from closing.

Cabo rises up from behind Laura and bellows a resonant sound unlike anything anyone has ever heard. The dog then slowly approaches, appearing to grow larger with every step. Another sound—a deep growl—resonates through the dog. The noise that reverberates through his body seemingly forms a word.

"*Leave!*"

Laura looks at the boys. She sees the fear in their eyes through the masks. The Jack-o'-lantern drops to the deck as the boys hurry off.

Laura quickly closes the door and looks at Cabo. She is both puzzled and relieved. She smiles at him. He wags his tail, walks over to her, and licks her hand.

* * *

It is a quiet Saturday morning. As Laura steps outside of the house, she notices several deep scratches on the inside of the screen door. She looks at the dog.

"Cabo, did you do this?"

The dog just looks at her.

"If you want to go outside, don't scratch the door." She shakes her head with disappointment.

Cabo continues to look at her for a moment, and then he walks over to the scratches and sniffs them.

Laura picks up the phone to call her mother only to discover that the phone is still dead. She grabs her cell phone and sees that she does not have a signal. She dismisses any concern and goes into the kitchen to make breakfast for herself and Cabo.

As Laura takes a scolding teapot off the stovetop, the doorbell rings. At the door, she sees a couple who appear to be in their late fifties. Both are smiling. She speaks through the door.

"Can I help you?" Laura asked.

The woman speaks.

"Hello, my name is Eileen McCleary, and this is my husband, Harold. We are your neighbors and we're here to welcome you."

"Oh, I'm sorry. Let me open the door."

Laura opens the door and greets the McClearys with a broad smile.

"Please, come in. My name is Laura."

The couple enters. Mrs. McCleary holds something wrapped in a kitchen towel. Cabo remains seated in the corner behind a shadow and never budges.

"We brought you a loaf of our fresh-baked bread."

"Oh, my! Thank you so much."

"That's quite all right. We love to see a new face. Has anyone else welcomed you to the neighborhood?"

"Yes, I already met the Parks family."

The McClearys look at each other.

"We don't know them," said Eileen. "What about the Bordeaux family?"

"No, I haven't."

"You'll find them interesting, I assure you."

Harold continues to remain silent.

"Well, I was about to make breakfast. Would you both like some tea?"

The woman sees the dog. "No thank you, we can't stay."

"Oh, there's no need to be concerned about my dog. He's very friendly, and smart."

"He looks like a remarkable animal, but we truly cannot stay."

As the McClearys leave, Laura quickly stops them.

"Eileen, I have to ask you about something. How long has your phone been out of service?"

"Out of service?" She briefly looks at Harold and then answers Laura. "Our phone is working perfectly fine."

* * *

In the morning, while Laura leaves for work, she sees Bill Parks. She calls out to him, but he doesn't seem to hear her.

While walking through Westry Plaza, Laura again sees the white-faced mime artist performing. He locks eyes with her and conveys a mean, contorted grimace.

* * *

The moon appears larger than normal in the starless night sky. Laura makes an attempt to finish the book that she recently started reading. She sits on the couch with Cabo's head cradled in her lap.

While turning the page, she hears rustling outside among some bushes. Then, she hears a loud thud. She looks out of the window and does not see anyone or anything. She looks at Cabo, who appears to be in distress. The dog runs upstairs despite Laura's calls to him. Then, the doorbell rings.

Laura returns to the window to see a family facing her from the bottom of the front porch. The gentleman, appearing to be the father, wears a narrow smile. She goes to the door, opens it, and steps outside.

"Good evening, young lady," said the gentleman. "We are the Bordeaux family. We live here. My name is Lucien. This is my wife, Henriette." He gestures to her.

"How do you do?" Laura said with a twitching smile. "My name is Laura, Laura Bennings."

"Also with us is Dolorès, Henriette's older sister." Lucien continues. "And, this is René, Henriette's younger brother."

Laura smiles at them. "Hello."

"And, finally, this is our young daughter, Eloise."

The little girl, who appears to be five years old, is holding a very dark, furry cat.

"Eloise, that's a beautiful name." Laura told her. "And, your cat is cute. What is his name?"

Eloise does not answer but, rather, offers Laura a blank look.

"Oh, well, um, would you like to come inside for some tea?" Laura said to everyone.

"No, thank you," said Lucien. "Henriette's father is at home and under our care."

"I'm sorry. Is he sick?"

"No, he is *ancient*."

Laura smiles. "Some other time, I hope."

Lucien smiles back. "We are very happy that you moved here. We will be watching over you. Again, good evening."

"Good evening," Laura said. She looks at the Bordeaux family as they walk off into the darkness. She regards their elegance as somewhat out-of-place and perhaps outdated.

FIVE

It has been a week since Laura met the Bordeaux family and she has not seen any of them since. The neighborhood in general has been unusually quiet and untroubled by any vehicle traffic.

Inside, Laura walks around the house in a long robe. At times, she feels like she is being watched. But, she quickly dismisses this every time the feeling arises.

While at the kitchen table, she writes a brief shopping list on a scrap of paper. "Bread, Coffee, Wine, Cake, Chocolate." The tea kettle whistles. She then crumples up the paper and addresses the whistling kettle. When she returns to the table with a mug of tea, the piece of paper that she crumpled up is lying there flat. She again crumples it up and, this time, throws it into the garbage pail.

* * *

Julia Bennings visits again. Her visit is unannounced.

"Laura, my baby, happy birthday!" Julia said as she entered. "Goodness, you've lost weight. I hope you've been eating right."

"Mom, I haven't lost weight." She takes the woman's coat. "Let me make coffee."

Laura hurries to the kitchen. She sees a scrap of paper on the table. She quickly throws it into the pail. The opens the cabinet and sees that she does not have enough coffee.

"Mom, I'm out of coffee. Would you like tea?"

"That's fine."

Laura carries a tray into the parlor and sets it down on a table. The women quietly take their cups and dig their spoons into the sugar bowl. Cabo lies at the other side of the room.

"Where did you find *him?*" Julia asked regarding the dog.

"We sort of found each other."

"Hmm. I don't know."

"Since when do you not like dogs?"

"I don't know. Couldn't you get a goldfish, or something less messy?"

Laura ignores her question and looks down at her cup. "Mom, I think the house is haunted."

"Which house?"

"*This* house. The house we're in right now."

"Oh, nonsense! If you feel something odd is happening, just light one of the candles that I gave you." Julia smiles.

"There have been some happenings."

"This is a nice house and it makes a fine home for anyone."

"Mom, what do you mean?"

"I was thinking a lot about what you said, and I think you were right."

"About what? Mom, you're not making much sense."

"Perhaps it was a good idea that you moved out. Maybe the time was right. Maybe I was holding you back."

Laura is surprised by her mother's reversal. "You weren't holding me back, mom. You were perfect."

* * *

Her office desk is cluttered with reports, documents, and illustration boards. They pile up daily—quicker than she can look them over. Despite the backlog, Laura stares blankly out of a wide window. Her morning hours were spent in meetings and with limited interactions with co-workers. Time seems to be moving slowly. She looks at her computer screen and notices that the screensaver is performing erratically.

Evan is nowhere to be found. Rumors are quickly abound that he was terminated. But, no one is saying anything for certain.

Laura leaves her office and goes to the basement. She quickly notices that the immense computer system known as Valerie has been removed. Where there were cables and wires are now holes in the walls; those cables appear to have been hastily torn out. She supposes that the virtual reality entertainment line has been dismantled, but there were no memos issued announcing this. She goes to Evan's office. She knocks, but no one answers. The door is locked.

Laura decides that it is time to get answers about Evan and the removal of Valerie. She takes the elevator up to see Nathaniel Westry. Westry's secretary sits at her desk with a smile on her face when Laura enters.

"Carol, I want to see Mr. Westry."

"I'm sorry, Miss Bennings, but Mr. Westry is on vacation."

"Well, can you tell me when he will return?"

"No, Miss Bennings, I cannot."

Laura is visibly upset at the secretary's undetailed explanation of Westry's whereabouts. She quickly leaves the office without speaking another word.

* * *

While at home, Laura wonders whether the Bordeaux family members are ghosts. She is also thinking about her mother's behavior during her recent visit. She also thinks of Evan.

Outside of her window, she sees Harold and Eileen McCleary. She calls out to them, but they continue on their way.

Cabo walks over to her. He curls up at her feet. She regards him as her only friend. She pets him gently. Under his thick fur, she feels scabs around his neck and back. Upon further inspection, she finds deep scratches. The dog looks into Laura's eyes as though he is trying to communicate his fear over whatever injured him.

Six

Laura wonders whether or not the game continues. She speculates that Valerie was dismantled only to be relocated to an undisclosed location. To test her theory, she plugs in her computer and attempts to enter the dark web to play the game. She encounters the same technical images as before. She types the same keys to log on. She presses the enter key.

>> *CODE NOT VALID* <<

Perhaps her theory is flawed, she thinks. She logs off and unplugs the computer.

Later that evening, Laura relaxes on a wide couch while slowly rubbing Cabo's neck. She wonders what has been scratching at his nose. One scratch over his eye looks rather deep. She considers that a raccoon or some other animal is trapped somewhere inside the house.

While in bed, she finishes some reading. She pulls up the covers, curls up slightly, and closes her eyes.

* * *

It is the next day. Laura awakens to peculiar noises coming from downstairs. Cabo, lying nearby, just looks at her. She rises from the bed and carefully walks down the steps. She begins to feel increasingly uneasy with every step that she takes.

In the dining room, Laura sees the entire Bordeaux family sitting around her dining room table. They appear to be in full swing of a lavish dinner party.

"Happy birthday, Laura!" they all shouted in unison immediately upon seeing her.

The surprise sends Laura into a daze. She attempts to form words, but the sudden stupor prevents her from moving her lips.

"Laura, let's have a seat," Henriette said as she assists Laura to a chair.

As Laura looks around, she feels as though she is not truly there; she does not think any of what she is experiencing is real. She shakes her head and attempts to communicate. She thinks for a moment that she is dreaming upstairs in bed, so she pinches both cheeks and pulls on them until she feels pain. She touches her teeth to make certain that they are all there and firmly in place. What compounds her feelings is the bizarre fact that no one seems to be reacting to her behavior. Everyone is merrily engaged in conversation. Their voices ricochet inside of her head and seem to echo down her body.

Laura looks down at the table. She does not recognize the elegant place settings and stemware.

As she slowly lifts her head, a colorful arrangement of foods of an elite caliber is carefully outspread before her on small plates over a laced tablecloth. All of the courses are served at once to all guests in strict Haute cuisine fashion. Each dish is uniquely elaborate and consists of meticulously prepared meats and vegetables in buttery sauces, with crusty breads, fresh fruit, and various cheeses. Fresh herbs and small flower pedals garnish several of the dishes. Tall bottles of Cabernet Sauvignon and Chardonnay grace the center of the table in a circle to form a crown.

Laura lifts her nose with hope that the odors will somehow allow her to come to her senses.

"Where did all this come from?" Laura managed to say. "How did you do this?"

"Oh, it's easy when you have the right ingredients," René said to Laura in an attempt to impress her.

Lucien clears his throat in René's direction. He appears to be a man in his fifties. He is lean, and he is dressed in the finest of clothes. Traces of gray hair above the ears give him a distinguished look, and his soft yet confident voice and refined facial and hand gestures make up the total of his persona.

"Laura, are you hungry?" Lucien asked with a caring smile.

Laura shakes her head.

"I see, perhaps later."

She slowly nods at him.

"Well," he continues, "You know my wife's sister, Dolorès." Lucien gestures to a heavyset frontierswoman sitting off to the side, chewing.

"Nice place," she said with food plainly visible in her mouth.

Lucien cringes at Dolorès' behavior as he continues his introductions. He motions toward Eloise who is wearing a lacey dress that would look good on any other little girl but, for reasons not fully known to Laura, the clothes look a bit off on this child.

"I believe you know my daughter, Eloise, and I hope that you do not mind that she brought her cat along. She goes everywhere with that cat."

Again Laura slowly nods at him.

"And you already met my wife, Henriette, and her charming brother, René."

Both Henriette—who looks to be in her forties, and René—perhaps in his thirties, present themselves as elegant and upscale as the patriarch. Laura continues nodding.

Lucien then walks over to a very old man dressed in a well-pressed, black suit seated at the head of the table. The man remains still and appears unresponsive. She focuses on his chest for a few moments, and is relieved to see it slightly rise and fall.

"Finally, Laura, this is my father-in-law, Ghislain Hauet."

Laura turns back to the cat. It is seated on Eloise's lap. Laura looks over its nearly-black fur down to the feathery tail. The cat, with deep green eyes, stares directly back at her. Their stares seem to interlock. Laura finds it unsettling as the stares linger on with either of them refusing to blink. The cat, however, is unfazed and shows no signs of concern over this contest.

"You never told me your cat's name." Laura asked Eloise at a level tone.

"Brick," Eloise answered rather bluntly.

Lucien sits down next to Henriette. He kisses his wife's cheek and opens a cloth napkin. "Oh, Laura," he explains, "You must settle down quickly and have children before it is too late."

"Lucien," Henriette interrupts with a friendly tone, "The good girl will find a man in her own time."

"Well, I am right here!" René said with a broad, rather gaudy smile.

"You must forgive my wife's younger brother," Lucien playfully interrupts. "René lacks self-control."

Dolorès, who appears to be older than Henriette, expresses her disgust in René's comment by throwing a piece of bread at him. René sheepishly giggles after the crust strikes him on the chest.

Laura ignores the misbehavior and looks over at Ghislain Hauet, who continues to sit quietly and gaze down at the table. Her eyes then wander back to the cat. She sees the feline wearing a seemingly evil stare. "Is this little bastard sizing me up?" she thinks. "I bet Cabo can tear the shit out him. I think I would like to see that."

"Laura!" Henriette said. "I called you a few times. Are you okay, darling?"

"I don't know. Your cat keeps looking at me." Laura looks around for Cabo. She looks up to see him at the top of the stairs, hiding but intently listening in on the activities.

"I hope you excuse Brick," René said. "There is no logical reason why he shouldn't like you. You're so beautiful. Well, he doesn't like me either if that makes you feel any better."

Laura continues to show discomfort.

"I'm sorry," René said. "I was only trying to cheer you up. Could I have a little smile? Maybe someday soon we could take a walk so we may get to know each other better."

"That's enough, René!" Lucien said as he slams his hand down on the table. He then quickly composes himself, strokes his hair and straightens his collar.

Dolorès appears deeply bored.

Laura cowers and shakes.

"Laura, please forgive my temper." Lucien said. "My child, we are together because we need something very important from you. We need your help. We wish to remain in town where we can watch over you."

Laura's mood changes very little. She sees that Ghislain Hauet continues to sit there and do nothing more than breathe. She is no longer certain if his sign of life comforts her. All that she wants is to burst out of there, but she feels frozen in place.

"Laura, I want you to trust me," Lucien continues. "There is no need for you to worry."

"Story time!" Eloise interrupts.

"Eloise, please?" Lucien scolded.

"But, Brick has a story to tell!" She puts her ear to the cat's face. "What's that, Brick? It's a special story just for Laura?"

"Go on, princess, tell us the story," Dolorès encouraged.

"Okay, this is the story of a dog named Sport. He was a smart dog and everyone loved him. He was sweet and friendly to all. However, he didn't like cats very much. So, one day, Sport was feeling very tired. And, he didn't want to eat. He became sicker and sicker until his neck swelled up like he was a bullfrog. So, he walked off alone into the forest where he shriveled up and died. The end."

Laura cringes. She tries to speak.

"Bravo!" Dolorès said as she applauds. "A wonderful story!"

"Eloise!" René said with a scalding tone as he sees Laura's reaction.

"René, I will not have you discipline Eloise," Lucien said with a stern voice. "You will know your place, young brother-in-law."

Laura tries to convey that it is all right. But, she struggles to form the words. One thing is very clear to her: She perceives Eloise as potentially dangerous.

Then, the room begins to spin for Laura. She keeps seeing each of their faces up close. So, she closes her eyes, but the spinning intensifies. She is overcome and passes out.

52

SEVEN

She believes that there is some force that prevents her from leaving the house.

This morning, Laura walked off with Cabo. She walked a great distance in a familiar direction only to find herself back home from the opposite direction.

Disturbed by this, even angered, she gets in her car and drives toward the main road. After a few minutes of driving, she finds herself pulling up to her house. Cabo sits at the front door watching her.

* * *

She attempts several times to call her mother, but she can't get through. The phone is still not working properly; this time there is a strange whistling sound coming from the receiver. Right after she hangs up, the doorbell rings.

The McClearys are standing at her door with a basket of food.

"Laura?" Eileen said. "It's us. We hope that you're hungry."

"I am, thank you! Please, come in. May I get you something? Coffee?"

"No, we're fine, thank you," Eileen said.

They all enter the parlor and sit. Laura takes the basket onto her lap, uncovers the food, and immediately eats.

"Please excuse me," Laura said with a mouthful.

"Oh, my!" Eileen said. "That's quite all right."

After a hard swallow, Laura clears her throat.

"My phone still doesn't work," she said as her face begins to harden.

"Poor dear. Well, you may use our phone any time you wish," Harold said almost lovingly.

"I have something else to tell you," Laura said as she chews more.

The McClearys study her face.

"There are people living in my house."

"Yes. *You* live in this house," Eileen said reassuringly.

"And they won't leave."

The McClearys look at each other with concern. They think that Laura may be close to insanity.

"Laura, who won't leave?"

"The Boudreauxs," Laura whispered.

"Oh, the Boudreaux family?" Eileen chuckled. "They're harmless."

"They held a dinner party for me."

"That's nice."

"But it didn't feel right. I couldn't move. I couldn't think! It's like I wasn't truly there," she said erratically while reflecting on what had happened.

Eileen turns to her husband and gestures to him. "We'll say goodnight now," she said as the couple gingerly stand. "We'll show ourselves out."

As the McClearys walk to the front door, Eileen turns to Laura with an uneasy look.

"Find some help, my dear," she said.

* * *

Laura lies on a couch. Her eyes are red from crying and lost sleep. As she rises, she sees René standing under an entranceway. Laura is startled.

"What are you doing here? How did you get in?"

"Which question do you want me to answer first?" he quipped.

"I want you to leave!"

"I'll go, but let's just talk for a moment."

Laura doesn't want him there, but she gives in while thinking that perhaps he can help her. She sits back down on the couch. René walks over toward her and sits in a chair. He sits straight and focused on her.

"Laura, I think you are special. This is the first time I can freely express myself to you..."

"I'm happy for you."

"You are unlike anyone I have ever met."

"My mother would love you."

"There is no one romantic in your life?"

"Does your Henriette know how uncouth you are?"

"Uncouth?"

"Yes, hasn't your sister ever taught you the proper way to court a lady?"

René offers a puzzled look. "Should I join you on the couch?"

"No, that's not what I mean. Don't you see that I'm in danger?"

"I would never let anything happen to you."

"You don't understand. I can't leave. My house phone doesn't work, and my cell phone doesn't work. Do you have a cell phone?"

"No, I do not."

"How can you not have a cell phone? Are you a ghost?"

"I am *real.*"

Laura opens a small table drawer and takes out a scrap of paper and a pencil. "I want you to call my mother and tell her to come and get me right away," she said as she scribbles. She nearly picks René up from the chair while handing him the paper.

"Okay, I will do my best," he said.

"Yeah, you do that," she hastily said as she practically pushes him out of the front door. She pauses at the doorway. "Take care, my love," she said to him with playful disingenuousness.

He nods at her and smiles.

Eight

The halls are quiet now. In a moment, the doorbell will ring again. When it does, Laura will again answer the door. And, again, no one will be standing there.

She sits on the wood floor in the parlor with Cabo lying next to her. She gently pets him. She wonders if he is hungry... Then, the doorbell rings. She considers staying on the floor. It rings again. She stands, walks to the front door and opens it. No one is there.

"Fuck you!" Laura called out. She walks out of the house well beyond the driveway. She stops after walking a considerable distance, and then she completely turns around. She does not see anyone in any direction. Her brain races to come up with a logical reason and settles on the probability that the doorbell has a short circuit.

Laura goes back inside and returns to the floor with Cabo. She pets his head and looks at him. She is concerned about the dog and afraid that he may be sick. He has not been eating much. And, once again, she finds scratches on his nose.

She knows that the nearby rooms are empty. Yet, she keeps hearing footsteps in there. She hears them again. Cabo does not react to the sounds. She then thinks the sounds are only in her mind.

"Did you hear that?" she asked the dog as she continues to pet him. "Cabo, where are we? How are we getting out of here? We don't belong here. Do we belong anywhere?"

Cabo looks at her and wags his tail.

Just as Cabo, Laura has not been eating. She just looks at food, but there is no appetite. She knows that she should eat. So, they go to the kitchen. Laura notices Cabo moving slowly.

In the kitchen, Laura sees that the chairs were moved. They are arranged in an illogical, circular pattern. She moves the chairs back to where they should be without saying a word while Cabo sits in the corner. She looks up at the clock and realizes that it is very early in the morning. Out of the window above the sink the sun is about to rise. She completely lost track of time. She pours dog food in Cabo's bowl. The dog merely looks at her and does not move from where he is sitting.

Moments later, while in the bathroom, Laura is about to wash. As she looks into the mirror, she quickly sees the image of an unfamiliar face. It appears and suddenly vanishes. She dismisses the vision and proceeds to brush her teeth. As she brushes, she notices blood gradually accumulate in her mouth. She can taste it. She spits, but she does not see any blood. The taste is suddenly gone. She continues brushing. Then, she hears a tiny sound from the sink below. She looks down and sees what appears to be a tooth. She ignores it and continues brushing. She hears another tiny sound, then another, and then another. She feels her teeth become increasingly loose with each of her brush strokes. She drops her toothbrush into the sink and reaches into her mouth. One by one, she removes her teeth. The amount to blood coming from her mouth increases with every pull. She looks down at a sink that is entirely red with teeth scattered in it and, out of frustration, she then punches the mirror shattering it to pieces. She stops, closes her eyes, and attempts to compose herself from the horrific ordeal only to find that she was in bed all along. She checks her teeth and finds them healthy and in place.

* * *

Laura is alone outside of the house. She is inspecting her birdhouse, which has been empty for some time. She hears a man's voice from behind her.

"Hey! How have you been?"

Unexpectedly, the man that she recently dated has returned. He appears slightly different. Although, Laura did recognize him by the gash on his cheek.

"I tried calling you but my calls haven't gone

through. Are you all right?"

"What are you doing here? Leave or I'll call the police."

She turns away from him and proceeds toward the front door.

"Wait!" He follows her and, as she enters the house, he makes his way inside. He grabs her wrist tightly as his face contorts. He shows his teeth. She quickly takes a letter opener from a desk and attempts to stab him in the neck with it. He grabs her other wrist and forces her to drop her weapon. Then, Cabo leaps from the dark corner of the room and bites the man's throat. The man jumps back. Blood pours over his hands. The man runs in terror before he can lose consciousness. Cabo joins Laura on the floor and puts his head in her lap. She embraces the dog and breaks down crying.

* * *

Laura sits quietly holding Cabo on the couch. The doorbell rings to break the silence. She answers the door abruptly because she expects no one to be there.

"Laura, how are you?"

"Oh, hello, Mr. and Mrs. McCleary. Please come in."

The couple enters the house. They are immediately concerned by Laura's poor physical condition.

"May we sit and talk?" Eileen asked.

"Yes, of course."

They sit and look at each other for a moment.

"Did you hear that?" Laura asked.

"Hear what?" Harold asked.

"In the next room."

"We don't hear anything, my child." Eileen said.

"It's the fucking Bordeaux family. I can hear them lurking around."

The McClearys look at each other.

"Have you been eating, or bathing?" Eileen asked.

"Why?"

"Laura, we are concerned about you."

"I'm fine! I just want these people out of my fucking house!"

"But, honey, the other rooms are empty," Harold said. "We're the only ones here. You don't see that?"

Before Laura can answer him, she faints.

* * *

She awakens on the couch. She thinks that she is alone. She looks around for Cabo. She turns, and Eloise is standing there holding Brick. Laura slowly and carefully rises.

"Why are there scratches on my dog, Eloise?"

Eloise does not respond, and she shows no emotion. She whispers in Brick's ear.

"Shall we pounce?"

The cat seems to nod in response.

Laura is so terrified that she cannot speak.

62

NINE

Determined to drive out of town, Laura walks Cabo into her car. She is not concerned about any of the belongings that she is leaving behind. She does not care about Westry Technologies. She only wants safety for her and the dog. She swiftly drives off as her tires kick up gravel.

After turning in the direction of a major roadway, and after feeling confident that she is finally free, she finds herself traveling in an unintended direction. She is suddenly uncertain about where she is going.

"The highway should be right up this road," she said. "I can't see the signs."

As she passes under evergreens and through a vast clearing, she finds herself back at the house. She breaks. Her hands slightly tremble on the steering wheel. She has a sinking feeling.

"Cabo, it looks like we're still in the fucking Land of Oz."

She pulls up into the driveway.

* * *

She storms inside of the house. René is standing in the middle of the parlor. He looks at her.

"I want answers," she demands. "What is this?"

"Laura, I want to help you. I see that you are suffering."

"No! I will not have that. I need to know what is going on."

The doorbell rings.

"God damn it!" Laura shouted. She throws open the door. "Evan?"

Evan stands in the doorway. He is about to speak, but he hesitates for a moment when he sees René. Evan points at him. "You, leave now," he ordered.

René quickly leaves without saying anything.

Laura grabs Evan by his shoulders. "You have to help me!"

"Okay, let's sit down for a moment."

"Is there a way out of here?"

"Just sit and I'll explain."

Evan sits next to her and looks into her eyes.

"Laura, I entered the game and learned what happened to you. I'm so sorry."

"What do you mean?"

"You're still in the game. You haven't left it since you started playing."

"What?'

"Everything that you see around you is the game platform. It's not real."

"But, I don't understand."

"The game serves as a portal into a central plane of consciousness, and it interconnects with other planes when the portal was opened. You opened the portal when you started playing the game. I have been circumnavigating the game looking for you."

"Evan, what are you talking about?"

"The game allows each player to escape the boundaries of the physical plane and enter an alternate plane where other players play the game as 'saviors of the universe'. As a result, anything from the alternate plane may punch its way into our world. I tried to warn Westry."

"English, please?"

"Anything entering onto the physical plane could possess great power, and it could mean the end of reality as we know it."

"How do you know all this?"

"I helped designed the game. But, I didn't fully realize its potential until I entered the game myself."

"What do we do now?"

"Well, the game has not gone public yet. So, go to the computer, open the game, and stop playing."

"Who are the Bordeauxs? Who are these people?"

"Not people. They are entities from another existence. They may appear to be human, but they are not. They are dangerous and they should be avoided."

"Why do they need me?"

"They need access to the physical plane in order for their powers to be fully realized, and they are using you to get there."

* * *

While Laura sits at the computer with Evan, René swiftly enters the room with Lucien, Dolorès, and Henriette.

"Lucien, there she is," René said.

"Laura, please move away from there," Lucien ordered.

"Don't listen to him," Evan insists. "You need to stop the game here and now."

Lucien, Dolorès, and René grab Evan. They pull him down to the floor.

"You must go back and unplug Valerie at Westry Technologies!" Evan cries out. "That will stop the game from fully going public."

Lucien grabs Evan by the neck and squeezes tightly. Evan goes limp and lifeless.

Henriette gasps.

Laura cries out.

"Hail to Nathaniel Westry!" Dolorès shouted.

Lucien turns to Laura. He straightens his clothes. "My child, don't cry," he said. "I will allow you to open a portal to the physical plane. However, you must take us with you. It is the only way for you to get home."

Ten

While confining herself to the parlor, Laura stares blankly into a corner of the room. The ceiling above her creaks; she hopes that sound is from Cabo walking around upstairs, but she is uncertain.

René enters the room.

"Get out!" she demanded.

"Wait! I want to apologize. I panicked, and I didn't know what to do. I am new to all this."

"What are you talking about?"

"I didn't know Lucien would kill your friend."

"Where is Evan? Is he really dead?"

"I don't know. Look, just do what Lucien tells you to do. It's the only way that we can be free."

"What do you mean *we*?"

"We. Don't you see? We can be together. We were meant to be."

"I don't know."

"I love you, and I want to be with you."

Laura thinks quickly. Perhaps she should continue to play along with hope that René will let his guard down. She smiles at him.

"Leave me, for now. I'm so tired."

She closes her eyes. He smiles at her as he leaves.

* * *

The doorbell awakens Laura. At the door, the McClearys are standing there. She quickly opens the door to let them inside.

"Laura, how are you feeling?"

"Please help me, Eileen!"

"What's wrong?" Harold asked.

"I am being held captive here. They refuse to let me go."

"Who, darling?" Harold asked.

"Them! They are here."

"Who, honey?" Eileen asked. "No one is here. It's just us."

"Oh, no! We're not alone. They are all over, and they are watching us right now."

"Laura, everything is going to be all right." Eileen said.

"Yes, everything." Harold said.

The McClearys move closer to her.

"You will help us, Laura." Eileen said. "You will help us leave this place."

"Eileen? Harold? You, too?"

"You must do exactly what Lucien tells you to do. You will help free us."

"No!" I will do nothing of the kind."

"But, Laura, you must," Harold insists. "It's the only way for all of us to be free."

"Fuck you!" Laura shouted.

The McClearys move even closer. They grab hold of Laura and bring her to the floor.

From within the shadows in the corner of the room, Cabo leaps out and bites down on Harold's hand. The dog holds on tightly as his teeth tear into flesh and bones. Harold screams in agony as he tries to free himself from the dog's powerful grip. With one kick from Eileen, Cabo is knocked back into a wall. As the dog tries to recover from the blow, the McClearys quickly make their exit.

Cabo then joins Laura on the floor. She holds him. Then, the entire house slightly shakes. It seems as though someone or something was angered. Laura holds Cabo tighter until the trembling stops.

* * *

The house has become entirely unlivable, and there seems to be no help from her captivity. Activities are on the rise: There are almost constant tapping and banging noises, lights flicker throughout the place, and foul odors are coming from all around.

Downstairs, Laura notices that the rooms seem somewhat larger than normal, and that they appear to be growing in size with each passing hour.

While upstairs, Laura goes to bed. On this night, the bed's height has slightly changed again.

This time, the bed is both shorter and lower than the previous night. Also on this night, the bedroom walls seem to have closed in a bit more. In the halls, the floors have become increasingly unleveled. She needs to lean on the walls wherever she walks about.

She literally feels the world close in on her. Then, she senses endless space surrounding her. All that she can do now is hold the dog close and think of her dwindling options.

"Cabo, there must be a way out. There must be a way out while we leave those bastards behind."

Eleven

"**M**aybe Philadelphia was a dream, and *this* is reality," Laura told Cabo.

The dog just looks at her and pants.

She misses her mother, and she knows her mother must be worried about where she is.

"Laura," Lucien said as he entered the room. "Have you made up your mind?"

She understands that by opening the portal to go home she would also unleash terror. She sees René standing behind Lucien.

"Not yet," she said. "I need more time."

"No, young lady. Your time is running out, I am afraid. If you wait too long, you will die."

René barely hides his displeasure with Lucien's option.

Lucien notices that Laura and René made eye contact. He turns to leave. "Come, René."

Both men disappear.

Laura rises and walks into the next room only to find that it is the same room. She walks over to a door, but she cannot open it.

"We're going to play *this* game now? You can do a little better than this!" Laura then walks upstairs to her bedroom. She still cannot gain access to her computer, and she knows that Lucien is holding her back from accessing it.

* * *

Ghislain Hauet materializes in a chair facing Laura. Laura is unfazed by what she sees. He studies her for a moment as though he is thinking about what to say.

"What the hell do you want?" she asked.

"My child, you are not living a linear existence."

"English, please?"

He rises from the chair. "We are in the repository of all of humanity's best-kept secrets. It is a place where time does not exist."

She thinks. "Go on."

"You departed from the physical plane, and you are now deep in the Mariana's Web—so deep that, technically, we are standing on the Akashic plane."

"Why is that so important to me?"

"All the knowledge of the universe resides in the Akashic plane. All matter and energy are digitally recorded there and serve as a repository of the past."

"So, who are you? You're not Ghislain Hauet?"

"No. I am the Record Keeper. I am an artificial intelligence program that polices the Akashic plane and addresses unauthorized access. I guard and control, and I maintain balance between all planes. However, you have inadvertently bypassed me and opened a portal into Grand Central."

"The station?"

"Yes, it is a station, of sorts. Grand Central is the central plane of consciousness that interconnects with other planes including the physical plane when a portal is opened. The entities exist in the Akashic plane, and that is where they must remain."

"The Boudreaux family."

"Yes. The entities want to use you to gain access to your world. That must not happen."

"Who are they?"

"Who? They are not a 'who'. They are not human. They are pure evil, my child. I suppose, in your world, you may regard them as a coven of witches, black magicians, or maybe far worse." The Record Keeper removes a special talisman from his coat pocket and hands it to Laura. "Here, take this."

"What do I do with it?" She takes it.

"You must secretly download it before you open the portal. Lucien should never see this."

"Then what will happen?"

"That, I am uncertain. It has never been done before. But, if it works correctly, only you should return home. Also, no one should ever know that I am the Record Keeper. If Lucien finds out, he could destroy me. Then, all would be lost."

"I understand," she said as her voice slightly trembled.

"Be careful. Only you must go back, and only you must close the portal for good."

"And what will you do?"

"I will be standing by until after you leave. I will have a lot of cleaning up to do."

<h1 style="text-align:center">TWELVE</h1>

The computer remains unplugged on her bedroom desk. Laura sits on the bed and stares at it while its blank screen stares back. She thinks it is time for her to try something. Anxiety fills her as she approaches the computer with the talisman in her hand.

There is a knock on the door.

"Who?" she asked.

"It's René. I have news."

"Come in."

René enters with a very disturbed look on his face. "Lucien is planning something with you."

"Tell me."

"Um, the guillotine."

"*What?*"

"A public guillotine. But that's only if you don't cooperate with him."

"How much time do I have?"

"I don't know."

"Then, leave. I need some time to prepare."

René attempts to kiss Laura on her lips. Laura pushes back.

"René, answer me. Are you one of them?"

"Who?"

"Are you an entity, like Lucien? Like Eloise?"

"Oh, no. I'm a player."

"A player?"

"Yes, a player."

Without hesitating, Laura punches René hard in the face. Her force is so great that the talisman she was holding becomes dislodged from her grip.

René falls backwards and on to the floor. The talisman strikes the door and falls to the floor. The door that the talisman struck slightly glows and warps for a moment. René recovers from the blow, picks up the talisman, and quickly leaves the room.

Before Laura can do anything, Dolorès enters. She confronts Laura with her sizable presence. Laura steps back. Dolorès offers a menacing grin. As Dolorès is about to speak, Laura winds her fist behind her head and unleashes a hard punch to Dolorès's nose. As a result, the woman steps back while clenching her face. She inspects her injury and sees blood flow steadily out of her nostrils and over her hands. Dolorès, with immediate fear and confusion escapes by jumping into the wall mirror. Upon seeing this, Laura then runs downstairs to pursue René.

Laura looks around at the bottom of the stairs. In the shadows and unseen by Laura, Brick crouches down low. Laura turns only to see the cat emerge with his long claws extended. He digs them deep into Laura's thigh as he takes aim for her throat. He swipes, but narrowly misses. Laura punches Brick's body not once but several times, but the cat merely looks back at her with his deep-green eyes in anticipation that she will make a fatal mistake.

Cabo appears from the next room and quickly takes hold of Brick and throws the cat to the floor. Brick springs back with powerful agility and bites hard on Cabo's front leg. The cat gruesomely tears into flesh while the dog yelps in pain. As Brick sees an opportunity to strike Cabo's neck, the determined dog recovers and firmly chops down on Brick. The dog feels a crunch deep in Brick's body as the cat's bones break under the force of the bite. Cabo then hurls the cat's limp body into a wall ensuring the creature's demise. When the body strikes the wall, the housewarming plaque that Laura's mother gave her dislodges from its nail, falls, and strikes Eloise on the head killing her instantly. Cabo lies down next to Laura. Laura holds him.

"No more play time," Lucien proclaimed from the shadows. He steps out and approaches Laura.

"You go fuck yourself!" she said.

"We can continue to play this game a little longer until you are dead. Or, you can be free and back home—where you supposed to be."

"No! Let's play this game some more. I'm getting used to it. In fact, I like this game. I think I want to stay a while longer."

"Laura, you do not have the luxury of time. Either you will sit there and bleed out or I will walk over and snap your neck. Either way, you will die."

René materializes and immediately steps in. He looks at Laura for a moment, and then turns to Lucien.

"Please, my brother-in-law," René pleads. "Spare her."

"Oh, René," Lucien said. "You are so young and so foolish. Love is pure to you, like a poem, or like a wildflower." Lucien puts his hand on René's shoulder. "You are so innocent. No, I have a better word: *naive*."

Lucien then embraces René. His hold gets increasingly tighter. René tries to free himself, but his efforts are useless. Lucien continues to squeeze René's body with great strength until both men hear René's back break. René's body becomes limp. Lucien then drops the crushed body to the floor and walks away.

Laura struggles to get to René.

"My jacket," René whispered.

Laura puts her hand inside his pocket and discretely takes back the talisman. Blood flows from René's mouth as he succumbs to his injury.

"Okay, you bastard," Laura said without looking up. "You win."

"Good! Time waits for no one. Let us be off."

Lucien helps Laura to her feet. He guides her upstairs back to the computer. After she plugs the computer in, he sits her down. The monitor turns on as he stands close to her.

She gains access to the game's website. As she is about to enter the access code, Lucien sees something in her hand.

"What is that?" he asked.

She stands and takes a defensive stance.

"Give that to me," he demanded.

"No."

"Give that to me, now."

The talisman unexpectedly emits a considerable glow. Lucien lunges at Laura's hand, but she swiftly moves back. Out of desperation, she throws the talisman into the computer screen. She receives a serious jolt that throws her back. A flash illuminates everything around the woman.

There is silence.

* * *

Laura awakens. She thinks that she is back in her house, on her bedroom floor. She is surprised to see red wine stains on her shirt. She carefully surveys her surroundings and notices that the computer is still on, but the monitor appears broken. She ignores the stiffness in her entire body and unplugs the computer.

Downstairs, everything seems restored. There appears to be no damage. Even her philodendron has not withered away. She thinks of Evan and looks around for him, but he is nowhere to be found. She's not sure how he is or if he was ever there.

She sees her car keys on the table. She grabs them and rushes out of the house. All she has on her mind as she leaves is that Valerie must be shut down back at Westry Technologies, and that she must do it fast.

EPILOGUE

She stands outside and watches as a well-packed moving truck drives off the property. In the driveway, Laura's car is filled with her belongings in the same cardboard boxes and milk crates as before. She pulls the front seatbelt across the well-grown philodendron, this time to keep the plant from falling over. She removes her birdhouse from the post and carefully packs it with her mother's plaque.

The latest *Harrogate News* newspaper sits by the doorstep. She picks it up and opens it. Inside, an article explains Evan Platt's death. His body was found in his apartment. It reads that he was the victim of a severe heart attack. The article says little more.

She finds it difficult to consider that the persons and surroundings that she encountered while in the game were not real. It was all virtual. Some things were merely interpretations or imaginative inputs of what she already knew, while other things, like members of the Bordeaux family, were living entities of pure evil.

If Nathaniel Westry's game went global, Evan had estimated that total human inhalation would have occurred within seventy-two hours.

* * *

"I hope you weren't planning on leaving without saying good-bye," Bill Parks said.

"I wouldn't think of it," Laura responded.

"You know, it's too bad we didn't get to know each other better."

"Well, I really wasn't happy with the house. I found a better one on Oaks Street not far from here. I had to take advantage of that opportunity."

From up the road, Lilian and Aaron walk up to the house. Lilian holds a cake box. The boy wears his arm in a sling.

"Aaron, what happened to you?" Laura asked.

"I fell out of a tree."

"He's either on the computer or climbing around," Lilian said with a playful smirk.

"Oh, Aaron, I'm so sorry you got hurt," Laura said.

"Here, Laura. Aaron and I baked you a chocolate cake with Bordeaux cherries."

"Bordeaux cherries?" Laura asked.

"That's right," Lilian said. "I hope you're not allergic."

"No, not at all. I love cherries." Laura receives the cake.

"We are so sorry to see you leave," Lilian said.

"I just told her that," Bill said. "Laura was just telling me that she bought a house on Oaks Street."

Laura leans into Aaron, almost in a whisper, "Yes, and it's a big, Victorian house with many rooms to hide. And it has a big porch to sit under in the summertime and drink lemonade. And there's a beautiful garden to plant flowers. I might even get a dog. If it's okay with your mom and dad, maybe you'll come and visit me?"

Bill and Lilian smile.

As the Parks couple walk off, Aaron stays behind and caringly looks at Laura.

"Miss Bennings, are *you* all right?" he asked.

"Yeah, I'm fine," she said with a puzzled look. "Why?"

"I was Cabo."

FORTHCOMING BY FRANCIS JOHN BALDUCCI

Voyage of the Behemoth
Cabbage Man
The Mongoose and the Serpent
The Devil's End

87

www.ingramcontent.com/pod-product-compliance
Lightning Source LLC
Chambersburg PA
CBHW061031050726
47592CB00004B/1398